TORRENT

Bernard Ashley

With illustrations by
Alan Brown

Barrington Stoke

For John and Wendy

First published in 2004 in Great Britain by
Barrington Stoke Ltd
18 Walker Street, Edinburgh, EH3 7LP

www.barringtonstoke.co.uk

This edition first published 2015

A CIP catalogue record for this book is available
from the British Library upon request

ISBN: 978-1-78112-454-3

Printed in China by Leo

CONTENTS

Chapter 1
A Fool

Tom was a fool to swim alone, but he'd got very hot on the long hike up the mountain – and the water of the Blue Dam looked so cool and clear.

Tom tore off his clothes and dived in – and in a second he went from much too hot to much too cold. Melting snow was running into the dam and the water hurt and crushed him and sucked the air from his lungs. He had to get back to the side. He had to swim, or go under.

"Kick your legs!" he told himself. "Work your arms! Get to the side before you freeze to death!" But his legs had gone dead and they hurt like hell. He had cramp. Killer cramp. Somehow, with his body blue, Tom kept on swimming. Just as everything went black, he grabbed at the bank. Somehow he had made it.

Tom pulled himself out. He rubbed some life into his legs and looked back at the dam.

TORRENT

The water was rising, higher and higher. The dam was so full that it was drowning everything. Even the flowers on the bank were under the water now. He took some photos of them. He was shaking so much it was hard to hold the camera still.

What a fool! He was lucky to be alive.

Back in his one-man tent down at the camp site, Tom looked at his phone. The flowers he'd seen under the water were called violas – Drowned Violas!

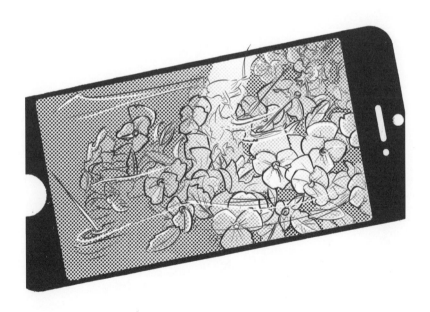

But how had Tom saved himself from drowning? In the icy water he'd been hit by cramp – and you can't swim with cramp. It was a miracle.

Chapter 2
A Dream

"Get out!"

"Run!"

"The dam's giving way!"

The sun was up. It was morning and people were yelling outside Tom's tent. They

were running and tripping on his tent pegs. What the hell was going on? Tom's head was still filled with a dream he'd had where he was swimming in the Blue Dam. He was with someone else – but who?

When Tom poked his head out of the tent, the camp site was almost empty. People were rushing for the road – on bikes and motorbikes, in cars and camper vans. They were racing each other to get away.

Tom saw the mountain stream across the field. It ran down from the Blue Dam. But it wasn't a stream any more, it was a river –

much wider than before and spreading

out across the grass. Twigs and branches,

bushes and bits of wood were rushing down

in the torrent.

"Come on! Run for it!" someone yelled. "Get on the lorry!"

Tom looked over to the gate of the camp site. The sheep farmer who ran the site had backed his lorry out of the barn and was ready to go. The lorry was packed with campers who didn't have cars or bikes.

"Come on!" People were yelling at Tom as the lorry started to move. Tom ran for it. The dam was giving way and the river was flooding the site. When the dam broke, the water would become a torrent – and he knew what that meant. It would carry rocks and trees down with it and would destroy everything in the valley. Anyone or anything in its way would be swept to their death. So Tom had to get to that lorry fast.

But as he ran, his dream still fresh in his head, he tripped over his own tent peg. When he got up, the lorry was pulling away. It revved off down the road before he could reach it.

Tom was left behind – alone with the rushing water, roaring as it rose. The road ran two miles down the mountain and out onto the plain. It ran between high rocks on

TORRENT

either side and across an old bridge at the bottom of the valley.

If Tom couldn't get down to the bridge before the water swept it away he would die. But how could he run two miles in time?

Tom was doomed. He had almost drowned in the Blue Dam. Now he would drown in the same water when it came rushing down. It was the end for him – but he had to *try* to save himself. He mustn't give up!

Tom started to run down the road. He
ran as he had never run before, his legs and
arms pumping.

The water was over the camp site now and coming down the road behind Tom. The sound of it roaring down the mountain was getting louder – and there were rocks in the racing water, bouncing like tennis balls. Soon there would be more rocks – much

bigger ones. And he couldn't even climb a tree because uprooted trees were rushing past him.

What was he going to do? He didn't have a hope.

Chapter 3
A Moto

But what was that other sound Tom could

hear over the rushing water? It sounded like

a motorbike.

   And it was a motorbike – coming

down the road from the camp site. A girl

was riding a moto – one of those small

motorbikes that the kids all rode.

'She must have been asleep in her tent like me,' Tom thought. He hadn't seen her on the camp site before, but she looked familiar. She rode up to him, and stopped.

"Get on, boy! Quick!" She was French, pretty, in a thin dress with bare legs.

"Thank you! Thank you!" Tom got onto the small seat behind her. It was a tight squeeze.

"Hold on tight!" she said.

So Tom held on tight around the girl's waist as she revved the engine and they bumped over the grass.

But she didn't make for the road. She headed for the trees.

"Where are you going?" Tom yelled.

"Road no good! River washes it away! There is a track!"

"Are you sure?" Tom asked. They seemed to be heading into thick forest.

"I know this track!" the girl shouted. "You come or not?"

"I come!"

This girl was his only hope. And Tom knew that she was right – the road would soon be swept away by the torrent. This other way was their best hope. A short cut to the bridge before it was swept away.

They raced into the trees. Tom had to hang onto the girl as they bumped along a narrow track. Thin branches hit his face and nettles stung his legs. He shut his eyes and put his head down. He couldn't see where they were going – but he had to trust the girl. And for a few moments Tom almost enjoyed hugging this girl tight as they twisted and bumped their way down the mountain.

The girl steered them into the forest. She leaned this way and that and Tom held tight onto her. When her body moved, he moved with her. She knew the track so well – she must have ridden it many times.

All of a sudden, the girl looked back. She shouted a French swear word. She had heard the same sound Tom had just heard.

Help! What was that, racing behind them?

Chapter 4
A Roller-coaster

It was water. Roaring water. Part of the flood had branched off and taken the same track as them. The same short cut. Tom could hear it behind them, crashing past bushes, bending trees.

"Water! Behind us!" he yelled.

"I know! I hear! Hold on tight!"

The girl did a sudden skid. The moto
went sideways and shot off the track. Now
they were away, riding past bushes and
nettles. They twisted and turned and almost
smashed into trees. Leaves, twigs and
branches hit them even harder. Tom could
only just hold on. He hugged the girl so
tight that they were like one person.

It worked! The flood didn't follow – it
stayed with the track. Tom and the girl shot
out into the open. But Tom's heart raced

when he saw where they were. His head went light.

No! Help! They couldn't do this!

They were at the top of a long, steep slope. They started to race down it – like the longest drop of a roller-coaster. They seemed to be falling head first down the mountain. Bushes and rocks were in the way – one mistake and they would be smashed to bits.

The girl twisted and turned the bike as they raced down. Tom clung on tight and went with her, this way and that. He could feel his heart thumping against her back,

knew his life was in her hands.

It was so exciting that Tom stopped caring about the danger. "Yeah!" he yelled.

Tom could hear the new flood raging past the trees – as well as the roar of the main torrent far off as it swept down the road. It was as if the mountain were a volcano and the water was racing lava.

And it was a race! They had to make it to the bridge before it was swept away.

And they had to make it without crashing.

The bike bounced – it bucked, it skidded, it swerved – but the girl held on. Then he saw below him the huge rocks on both sides of the gap at the end of the valley. There was just the last stretch of the road to go to the bridge. The bridge was still there, still

standing. But for how long? The mountain had become a torrent of water.

Could they make it? They had to! If not, they were dead.

Chapter 5
A Car

The girl raced for the last bit of road like the bravest of horse riders or the fastest of motorbike champs.

The roar was incredible. The dam had broken. It seemed that half the mountain was coming down in the torrent. It would

smash the bridge to pieces.

As the girl skidded the moto onto the

road, the tarmac began to shake under the

wheels. Huge cracks appeared. But there, in front of them, was the bridge. People were running to get away.

Tom had held the girl tight all the way down. Now, for extra speed, he lifted himself from the saddle, leaned forward over her, took the handlebars with her and willed the moto to race faster.

The moto shook on the cracking road – but with two pairs of hands Tom and the girl held it steady, racing for the bridge.

Behind them the torrent roared with a sound like the end of the world. The rocks loomed over them on both sides, forcing the water higher, faster, in a killer wave. In seconds the bridge would be smashed to bits and swept away.

But now the moto was on the bridge –
which was shaking with the force of the water.

20 metres, 15 metres, 10 metres – would
they make it? The shaking had become a

rocking. It was all they could do to hang on as the raging waters ran under them, flooding up and over the road.

Five metres to go! If the engine got flooded, it would pack up and they would be swept away in seconds.

But with Tom leaning over and the girl bending low, they made it to the other side. Just.

The girl twisted the handlebars hard to the left and shot up a side track onto higher ground, just as the great wave of water hit

TORRENT

the bridge and swept it away. Crash!
Splinter! Roar!

Down came the torrent. Trees, rocks,
fences and bits of barn twisted and jumped
in the racing water. There was a car and
tents and dead sheep in the angry waters.

The moto went up the track to higher
ground. People had gathered in the gardens
of a big house. Tom and the girl came off
the moto and fell onto the dry grass.

TORRENT

Chapter 6
Viola

Tom shut his eyes and thanked God that he was still alive.

He thanked God, and the girl. What skill! What bravery!

He opened his eyes and turned to thank her, to shake her hand, perhaps to kiss her. He would like to kiss her.

But she wasn't there. The moto was lying on the grass, but there was no sign of her. Tom looked around. People had blankets round them and mugs of hot coffee in their hands. Some were crying with shock. Others were looking for friends from the camp site and the farms. But the girl wasn't there.

Tom asked everyone – but they all told him the same thing. The same chilling thing.

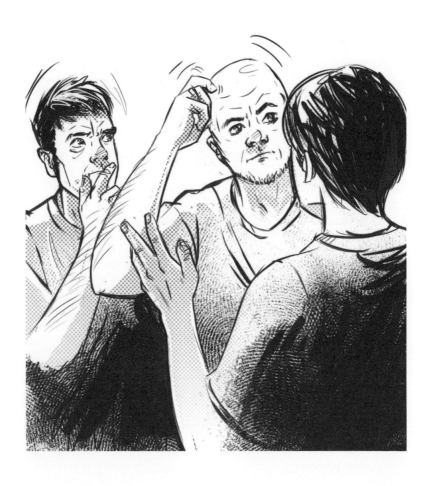

She had never been there. No one had seen her. Tom had ridden into the garden on his own.

On his own? Did they think he was a fool? Was it some sort of joke? He didn't even know how to ride a moto.

A man said Tom was in shock. He said he must have been so scared that he couldn't remember what he'd done. Everyone was so sure that Tom had ridden into the garden on his own that he almost started to believe it himself.

Until the sheep farmer from the camp site saw the moto.

"Who brings this?" he yelled. "Who steals my girl's moto?"

People pointed at Tom. The farmer came over to him. 'He's going to hit me,' Tom thought. But he didn't.

"Thank you," he said. "You save her moto from the barn. And the barn is ..." He was close to tears. "... Smashed and swept away – with my camp site."

"No," said Tom. "She saved the moto. And she saved me."

But the farmer looked at him with a hurt face.

"Not funny!" he said. "Do not make this joke!"

"It's not a joke," Tom told him. "It's true. She rode up to me and told me to get on the back ..."

The farmer's hands dropped to his sides. He stared at Tom. "And how can she do this?" he said. "She is dead. Five years, she is dead. I keep her moto because she loved it. It is all I have left of her ..."

Tom stared back. He had gone cold. Colder than in the Blue Dam. He could hardly ask what he needed to ask.

"How did she die?" But he knew the answer.

"In the Blue Dam," the farmer said. "She swims alone, it is too cold, and she dies ..."

Tom wanted to drop to the ground. His legs would give way any second. Because now he knew who it was in his dream. He

knew who had helped him swim to the bank of the dam where the drowned flowers grew.

The girl. The dead girl.

Tom looked into the farmer's eyes.

"And what was her name?" he said softly.

"Viola," the farmer said. "My girl was Viola."

And somehow Tom had known that too.

Drowned Viola of the Blue Dam.

Our books are tested
for children and young people by
children and young people.

Thanks to everyone who consulted on
a manuscript for their time and effort in
helping us to make our books better
for our readers.

More from *Barrington Stoke* ...

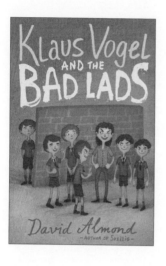

Klaus Vogel and the Bad Lads
DAVID ALMOND

The fire at Mr Eustace's happens the same week Klaus Vogel arrives. A scrawny kid from East Germany. A new target for Joe.

But Klaus Vogel will change things forever for the Bad Lads.

Respect
MICHAELA MORGAN

Tully and his brother don't have much. But they do have each other. And Tully has an amazing talent.

Football.

But then the First World War begins, and Tully goes on the earn respect of a different kind.

Based on the amazing true story of Walter Tull, a First World War hero.

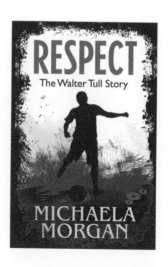

Six Hours
PETE JOHNSON

Every teenager should be allowed to take six hours off ... and just chill. That's what Lara thinks. No wonder she is always in trouble. Dominic has never done anything wrong in his life. But Lara encourages him to escape from school with her. Six hours of freedom stretch before them. Six hours they will never forget.

Jon for Short
MALORIE BLACKMAN

As the blade flashed down in the dim light, it seemed to wink, wink, wink ... Arms came up to ward off the flashes of light, but it did no good. The flashes got harder and faster. Jon is in hospital. He can't move. The doctors have taken his arms and he is sure his legs are next. Will Jon ever escape?

www.barringtonstoke.co.uk